For my mother, who taught me how to read. — V.D.P.

For my family. — M.J.

For Cara, Ramona, and Madeline. — B.M.

Brer Rabbit

JUMP!

The Adventures of Brer Rabbit

BY JOEL CHANDLER HARRIS

ADAPTED BY VAN DYKE PARKS AND MALCOLM JONES

ILLUSTRATED BY BARRY MOSER

Voyager Books

Harcourt Brace & Company

San Diego   New York   London

Requests for permission to make copies of any part of the work should be mailed to:
Permissions Department, Harcourt Brace & Company, 6277 Sea Harbor Drive,
Orlando, Florida 32887-6777.

First Voyager Books edition 1997
Voyager Books is a registered trademark of Harcourt Brace & Company.

Library of Congress Cataloging-in-Publication Data
Parks, Van Dyke.
Jump!: the adventures of Brer Rabbit.
"Adapted from folktales collected by Joel Chandler
Harris" — Added t.p.
Summary: A retelling of five folktales in which
crafty Brer Rabbit tries to outsmart all the other
creatures in the animal community.
1. Afro-Americans — Folklore. 2. Tales — Southern
States. [1. Folklore, Afro-Americans. 2. Animals —
Folklore] I. Jones, Malcolm, 1952–   II. Moser,
Barry, ill. III. Harris, Joel Chandler, 1848–1908.
Adventures of Brer Rabbit. IV. Title. V. Title:
Adventures of Brer Rabbit.
PZ8.1.P2255Ju 1986   398.2'452 86-7654
ISBN 0-15-241350-2
ISBN 0-15-201493-4 (pbk.)

Printed in Singapore

F E D C B A

The illustrations in this book were executed with watercolor and ink on Fabriano Classico.
The text type was set in Cochin by Thompson Type, San Diego, California.
The display type was set in John Peters' Castellar by Pennyroyal Press, West Hatfield, Massachusetts.
Color separations were made by Heinz Weber, Inc., Los Angeles, California.
Printed and bound by Tien Wah Press, Singapore.
This book was printed on Leykam recycled paper, which contains more than
20 percent postconsumer waste and has a total recycled content of at least 50 percent.
Production supervision by Warren Wallerstein and Ginger Boyer
Designed by Joy Chu and Barry Moser

Contents

Storytellers' Note

People will talk, and as long as they do, they will tell each other stories. The origin of these particular stories is complex and uncertain. In Jamaica, for example, "Brer Rabbit Grossly Deceives Brer Fox" is told about Tiger and Anansi the Spider.

Whatever their history, we know these tales were told by black slaves in the American South, who came to the United States against their will, with little besides the words in their mouths. These stories were first told aloud to the whole community, and the lighthearted mischief in them has great appeal to all ages. Nowhere will you find a better example of pluck and cleverness triumphing over brute strength.

When Joel Chandler Harris, a Georgian newspaperman, collected and recorded these tales in the late 1800s, they were very popular. Harris took great care to present the stories in the dialect of nineteenth-century black storytellers. In his book *Uncle Remus: His Songs and His Sayings*, Harris created a character named Uncle Remus, an elderly black plantation slave who told stories about Brer Rabbit and his friends to a little white boy.

Harris has been both applauded and deeply criticized for his portrayal of life in the Old South. But the lessons in these stories are universal, and there are few corners in life that they do not illuminate. Tempered by hardship and nourished by hope, these tales are a testament to the belief that no one can be wholly owned who does not wish it.

— V.D.P.
— M.J.

JUMP!

The Adventures of Brer Rabbit

Dk Moon

The Comeuppance of Brer Wolf

WAY back yonder when the moon was lots bigger than he is now, when the nights were long and the days were short, with plenty of wood on the fire and sweet potatoes in the embers, Brer Rabbit could outdo all the other creatures.

He was born little, so no matter whereabouts you put him, he could cut capers and play pranks. What he couldn't do with his feet he could do with his head, and when his head got him in trouble, he put his dependence back on his feet, because that's where he kept his lippity-clip and his blickety-blick.

Back then, Brer Wolf and Brer Fox were always laying traps for Brer Rabbit, and day in and day out, they did all that they could, they did, to catch him. Finally there came a time when Brer Rabbit got no peace whatsoever. He could not even leave his yard, for fear that Brer Wolf would raid his house and make off with some of the family to put in the stew pot.

Brer Rabbit built a straw house, and Brer Wolf tore it down. He built a house of pine-tops. That went the same way. Then he built a house out of bark. That was raided in the same fashion. And every time Brer Rabbit lost a house, he lost one of his children as well.

At last Brer Rabbit got mad, he did. He went out and found some carpenters, and he hired them to build him a plank house with rock foundations. He had a hole made in the cellar where his children could hide when Brer Wolf was in the neighborhood. And he put a latch on the door so they could lock it from the inside.

After that, Brer Rabbit had some peace and quiet. He came and went as he pleased, and passed the time with his neighbors. Then he came home to sit by the fire and smoke his pipe and read the newspaper just the same as anyone.

When Brer Wolf saw all this, he lay low. The little rabbits were still mighty skittish, but it got so that cold chills didn't run up Brer Rabbit's spine anymore when he heard Brer Wolf gallop by.

By and by, one day Brer Rabbit heard a monstrous fuss and clatter up by the big road. And almost before he could get his ears fixed to listen, Brer Wolf ran in the door.

The little rabbits ran into the cellar, they did, quicker than blowing out a candle.

Brer Wolf, he was fairly covered with mud, and mighty nigh out of wind.

"Save me, Brer Rabbit," said Brer Wolf, said he. "The dogs are after me, and they'll tear me up! Don't you hear 'em coming? Oh, do please save me!"

"Jump in that chest, Brer Wolf," said Brer Rabbit, said he. "Jump in and make yourself at home."

In jumped Brer Wolf, down came the lid, and into the clasp went the hook.

Then Brer Rabbit went over to the looking glass and winked at himself. He drew the rocking chair in front of the fire, he did, and he took a big chaw of rabbit tobacco.

He sat there like that for a long time, rocking and thinking, thinking and rocking, working his thinking machine.

BERKWolf

Brer Rabbit Prepares His Plan

By and by, Brer Wolf said, "Them dogs gone, Brer Rabbit?"

"Seems like I hear one smelling 'round the chimney corner just now," Brer Rabbit said, said he. And he filled his kettle with water and put it on the fire.

"What're you doing now, Brer Rabbit?" asked Brer Wolf.

"I'm fixing you a cup of tea, Brer Wolf."

Then Brer Rabbit got out his drill and began boring little holes in the lid of the chest.

"What're you doing now, Brer Rabbit?"

"I'm boring some holes so you can breathe, Brer Wolf."

Brer Rabbit threw some more wood on the fire, and he told Brer Wolf, "I'm chunking up the fire so you won't get cold." And then he went into the cellar and fetched his children upstairs.

"What're you doing now, Brer Rabbit?"

"I'm telling my children what a nice fellow you are, Brer Wolf."

The little rabbits had to clap their hands over their mouths to keep from laughing.

Then Brer Rabbit took the kettle off the fire and began to pour the boiling water on the chest lid.

"What'm I hearing, Brer Rabbit?"

"You hear the wind blowing, Brer Wolf."

The hot water began to drip through the lid.

"What's that I feel, Brer Rabbit?"

"You feel your fleas biting, Brer Wolf."

"They're biting mighty hard, Brer Rabbit."

"Turn over on your other side, Brer Wolf."

"What's that I feel now, Brer Rabbit?"

"More fleas, Brer Wolf, more fleas."

"They're eating me up, Brer Rabbit!"

And those were the last words out of Brer Wolf for many a long hour. When he finally managed to light out of there that night, he was a wiser wolf, he was, and he wouldn't be back for a mighty long time.

The scalding water had done its business.

BICK Wolf Requited

BICK FOX

Brer Fox Goes Hunting but Brer Rabbit Bags the Game

AFTER Brer Fox heard how Brer Rabbit tricked Brer Wolf, he steered clear of Brer Rabbit. There was an abundance of times that Brer Fox could have nabbed Brer Rabbit, but every time he got the chance, he thought back to Brer Wolf, and he let Brer Rabbit alone.

By and by, they began to get more friendly with one another, like they used to be, and it got so Brer Fox would call on Brer Rabbit. They'd sit and smoke their pipes, they would, like no harsh feelings had ever rested betwixt them. But Brer Rabbit, he didn't forget how Brer Fox had dragged off a few of his children.

One day Brer Fox came along all dressed up and asked Brer Rabbit to go hunting. But Brer Rabbit, he was feeling lazy, and he told Brer Fox he had other fish to fry.

Brer Fox was mighty sorry, but he believed he'd go anyhow, and off he put.

He was gone all day. He had a monstrous streak of luck, and he bagged a sight of game.

By and by, towards evening, Brer Rabbit got up and stretched himself. It was almost time for Brer Fox to be getting home. Brer Rabbit mounted a tree stump, to see if he could see Brer Fox coming, and soon he spied him coming through the woods, singing like a fool at a frolic.

Brer Rabbit leapt off his stump bookity-bookity, and he lay down in the road and made like he was dead.

Brer Fox came along, he did, and saw him lying like that. You'd think he'd notice it was Brer Rabbit, but no, he just turned him over, he did, and examined him. Then he said, "This here rabbit is dead, and he looks like he's been dead a long time. But he's a mighty fat dead rabbit. He's the fattest rabbit I ever saw. But maybe he's been dead for too long. I'm afraid to take him home."

Brer Rabbit, he didn't say a thing, and Brer Fox, he sort of licked his chops, but he went his way and left Brer Rabbit lying in the road.

As soon as Brer Fox was out of sight, Brer Rabbit hopped up and dashed off through the woods to get ahead of Brer Fox again. When Brer Fox came up, there lay Brer Rabbit, looking cold and stiff.

Brer Fox looked at Brer Rabbit, and after studying things for a while, he unslung his game bag. "These rabbits are going to waste," he said. "I believe I'll leave my game bag here and go back for that other rabbit. I'll make folks believe I'm old man Hunter from Huntsville," said he.

With that, he dropped his bag of game and loped back up the road for that other rabbit. No sooner was he out of sight than old Brer Rabbit snatched up Brer Fox's game bag and put out for home.

The next time he saw Brer Fox, Brer Rabbit hollered out, "What'd you catch the other day, Brer Fox?"

Brer Fox sort of combed his flank with his tongue, and he hollered back, "I caught a handful of hard sense, Brer Rabbit," said he.

When he heard that, Brer Rabbit laughed. And then he said, "If I'd known that's what you were hunting, Brer Fox, I'd have loaned you some of mine."

Well, when Brer Fox saw how slick the trick worked for Brer Rabbit, he thought he'd try the same game on somebody else. So he watched for his chance, he did.

Brer Fox Studies the Situation

Bier Fox Meets Mr. Man

By and by, one day he heard Mr. Man coming down the big road in a one-horse wagon carrying some chickens and some eggs and some butter to town. Brer Fox heard him coming, he did, and he lay down in the road in front of the wagon. He lay still as could be, even when it looked like the horse's hoof was mighty nigh to smashing his nose.

When they got almost to Brer Fox, the horse shied, and Mr. Man hollered, "Whoa!" Then he looked down and saw Brer Fox lying there. He looked dead enough to be skinned. When Mr. Man saw that, he hollered out, "Heyo! There's the chap's been stealing my chickens and eating my pigs. Somebody's killed him, and I wish they'd killed him a long time ago."

Mr. Man looked around to see what the reason for this dead fox could be. But he didn't see anything, or hear anything, so he sat thinking for a while. By and by, he climbed out of the wagon, to better examine this fox, to see what had caused his death.

He felt Brer Fox's ear, and Brer Fox's ear felt warm. Then he felt Brer Fox's neck, and it felt right warm, too. He felt Brer Fox in the short ribs. Brer Fox was all right in the short ribs. Then he felt Brer Fox's legs. Brer Fox's legs were sound. He turned Brer Fox over, and lo and behold, Brer Fox was right limber.

When Mr. Man saw that, he said to himself, said he, "Heyo, there! How come this chicken-nabbing, pig-plucking rascal looks dead? There's no bones broken, and I don't see any blood. More than that, he's warm and limber. Something's wrong here, for sure! He might be dead. Then again he mightn't. But I'll just give him a whack with my whip handle to make sure."

With that, Mr. Man drew back and fetched Brer Fox a clip behind the ears — *pow!* The lick came so hard and so quick that Brer Fox thought he was a goner for certain. But before Mr. Man could draw back to fetch him another swipe, Brer Fox scrambled to his feet and made tracks away from there.

And that's what Brer Fox got for playing Mr. Smarty and copying after other folks.

Brer Fox Makes Tracks for Home

Brer Terrapin

Brer Rabbit Finds His Match

IF you've gotten the notion that Brer Rabbit is about the smartest creature in the whole of creation, you are mighty mistaken, because every once in a while something or other would happen to take the starch out of him.

It always happens that way. Go where you will and when you may, and stay as long as you choose to stay, and right there and then you'll surely find that folks who are full of conceit and proudness are going to get it taken out of them.

Brer Rabbit did get caught up with once, and it cooled him right off.

One day while Brer Terrapin was going down the big road, along came Brer Rabbit, full of rascality, a-lippity-clippity. He stopped when he reached up with Brer Terrapin, sat down and scratched for fleas, and after the two had passed the time of day with one another, they fell to disputing this and that. Before long, they got to arguing about which of them was the swiftest.

Brer Rabbit, he said he could outrun old Brer Terrapin, and Brer Terrapin, he vowed he could outrun Brer Rabbit.

Up and down they had it, until the first news you know, Brer Terrapin said he had a fifty-dollar bill in a chink in the chimney back home that said he could beat Brer Rabbit in a fair race.

Then Brer Rabbit said he had a fifty-dollar bill that told him that he could leave Brer Terrapin so far behind that he could sow some barley as he went along, and it would be ripe enough to cut by the time Brer Terrapin passed that way.

Anyhow, they made the bet and put up the money, and Brer Turkey Buzzard, he was summoned to be the judge and the stakeholder. It wasn't long before all the arrangements were made. The race was a five-mile heat, the ground was walked off, and at every mile a post was stuck up.

Brer Rabbit was to run down the big road, and Brer Terrapin, he said he'd run through the woods. Folks told him he could get along faster in the road, but Brer Terrapin, he knew what he was doing.

Miss Meadows and the gals, who were neighbor ladies down the lane, got wind of the fun. So did most of the other folks, and when the day was set, they determined to be on hand.

Brer Rabbit trained every day, and he skipped over the ground just as gaily as a june bug. Brer Terrapin, he lay low in the swamp. He had a wife and three children, and they were the spittin' image of the old man. Anyone who knew one from the other had to take a spyglass to do it, and even then they were likely to get fooled.

That's the way matters stood on the day of the race. On that day, Brer Terrapin and his wife and his children got up and went to the track. His wife took up her stand next to the first milepost. The children each took a place down the line at the other mileposts, up to the last, and there Brer Terrapin took his stand.

By and by, folks came: Judge Buzzard, he came, and then came Miss Meadows and the gals, and then came Brer Rabbit, with ribbons tied around his neck and streaming from his ears.

The folks all went to the other end of the track to see how the race would come out.

When the time came, Judge Buzzard strutted around and pulled out his watch, and then he hollered, "Gents, you ready?"

Brer Rabbit hollered back, "Yes," and Mrs. Terrapin hollered, "Go"

Brer Judge T. Buzzard

The Day of the Race

from the edge of the woods. Brer Rabbit, he lit out, and Mrs. Terrapin, she put out for home. Judge Buzzard rose and skimmed along to see that the race was run fair.

When Brer Rabbit got to the first milepost, one of the terrapin children crawled out of the woods and made for the post.

Brer Rabbit, he hollered out, "Where are you, Brer Terrapin?"

"Here I come a-crawling," said the terrapin, said he.

Brer Rabbit was so glad he was ahead that he put out harder than ever, while the terrapin, he put out for home.

When Brer Rabbit reached the next post, another terrapin crawled out of the woods.

"Where are you, Brer Terrapin?"

"Here I come a-boiling," said the terrapin, said he.

Brer Rabbit, he lit out, he did, and when he came to the next post, there was a terrapin.

Brer Rabbit had one more mile to run, and by then he felt sort of wheezy.

About that time, Brer Terrapin looked back down the road and saw Brer Buzzard sailing along, and he knew his turn was up. So he scrambled out of the woods, rolled across the ditch, and shuffled through the crowd so that he could get to the milepost and crawl behind it.

By and by, along came Brer Rabbit. He looked around, and when he didn't see Brer Terrapin, he hollered out, "Gimme my money, Brer Buzzard, gimme my money!"

Old Brer Terrapin, he raised up from behind the post and said, said he, "If you'll give me time to catch my breath, gents and ladies, I 'spect I'll finger that money myself."

Then Miss Meadows and the gals, they hollered and laughed fit to kill themselves.

Sure enough, Brer Terrapin tied the purse around his neck and skedaddled off for home.

Of course, that was cheating, and the creatures had begun to cheat, and then the folks took it up, and it kept appearing. It's mighty catching, so you watch yourself, that somebody doesn't cheat you before your hair turns gray.

Brer Rabbit in the Agony of Defeat

Miss Molly Cottontail

Brer Rabbit Grossly Deceives Brer Fox

SEEMS like the tale about how Brer Rabbit got outrun by Brer Terrapin got talked up amongst the neighbors. Brer Fox, he talked the loudest, leastways he did when he dropped in on Miss Meadows, Miss Molly Cottontail, and the rest of the gals.

The next time Brer Rabbit came to visit, Miss Meadows tackled him about it, and the gals set to laughing so hard their sides nearly split.

Brer Rabbit sat just as cool as a cucumber, he did. By and by, he crossed his legs, and winked his eye slow, and he said, "You may believe me or not—goodness knows I ain't fittin' to tell no tale. But Brer Fox was my daddy's riding horse for thirty years that I know of," said he. Then he paid his respects and off he marched.

The next day, Brer Fox came to visit, and when he began to laugh about Brer Rabbit, Miss Meadows and the gals up and told him what Brer Rabbit said.

Then Brer Fox grit his teeth sure enough, he did, and he looked mighty grumpy. But when he rose to go, he up and said, "I ain't disputing what you say, but I'll make Brer Rabbit chew up his words and spit 'em out right here where you can see 'em."

And with that, off Brer Fox put.

When he got to the big road, he shook the dew off his tail, and made a straight shoot for Brer Rabbit's house. When he got there, Brer Rabbit was expecting him, and the door was locked tight.

Brer Fox knocked. Nobody answered. Then he knocked again— *Blam! Blam!*

Then Brer Rabbit hollered out mighty weak, "Is that you, Brer Fox? I want you to run and fetch the doctor. That bit of parsley I ate this morning is getting away with me. Please, Brer Fox, run quick."

"I've come after you, Brer Rabbit," said Brer Fox, said he. "There's a party up at Miss Meadows's, and all the gals'll be there, and Miss Molly Cottontail allowed as how it ain't no party 'less I fetch you," said Brer Fox, said he.

Brer Rabbit's House in the Briar Patch

Then Brer Rabbit said he was too sick, and Brer Fox said he wasn't, and there they had it up and down, disputing and contending. Brer Rabbit said he couldn't walk. Brer Fox said he'd carry him. Brer Rabbit said how. Brer Fox said in his arms. Brer Rabbit said he might drop him. Brer Fox said he wouldn't.

By and by, Brer Rabbit said he'd go if Brer Fox would carry him on his back. Brer Fox said he would. Brer Rabbit said he couldn't ride without a saddle. So Brer Fox said he'd get a saddle.

Then Brer Rabbit said he couldn't sit in a saddle without a bridle to hold. Brer Fox said he'd get a bridle. Brer Rabbit said he couldn't ride without a blind bridle, because Brer Fox would shy at the stumps along the road and fling him off. Brer Fox said he'd get a blind bridle. Then Brer Rabbit said he'd go.

Brer Fox said he'd give Brer Rabbit a ride up to Miss Meadows's most of the way, and then Brer Rabbit could get down and walk the rest of the way, so Brer Fox wouldn't embarrass himself. And Brer Rabbit agreed to that. So Brer Fox leapt off to get the saddle and bridle.

Of course, Brer Rabbit knew that Brer Fox was fixing to play some trick on him. He always was. No more than a week ago, Brer Fox tried to drag off two of the baby rabs.

Now Brer Rabbit determined to outdo him again. By the time he combed his hair and twisted his mustache and got himself fixed up, there came Brer Fox, saddle and bridle on, looking pert as a circus pony. He trotted to the door and stood pawing the ground and chomping a bit just like a real horse. So Brer Rabbit mounted, he did, and they ambled off.

Brer Fox couldn't see behind himself with the blind bridle on, but by and by, he felt Brer Rabbit raise one of his feet.

"What you doin' now, Brer Rabbit?" said he.

"Shortening the left stirrup, Brer Fox."

By and by, Brer Rabbit raised the other foot.

"What you doin' now, Brer Rabbit?"

"Pulling up my pants, Brer Fox," said Brer Rabbit.

But all the time he was putting on his spurs.

When they got close to Miss Meadows's place, they reached the spot where Brer Rabbit was supposed to get off, and Brer Fox stood still. He was thinking how good his rabbit stew would taste for supper.

The Rabbit Family's Riding Horse

Just then Brer Rabbit slapped those spurs into Brer Fox's flanks, and you best believe Brer Fox covered some ground.

When they got to the house, Miss Meadows and all the gals were sitting on the piazza. Instead of stopping at the gate, Brer Rabbit rode on by, he did, down the road to the horse rack, where he hitched up Brer Fox.

Brer Rabbit sauntered into the house and shook hands with the gals and sat down. He lit his cigar same as any city slicker, he did. By and by, he drew in a long puff and let it out in a cloud, and then he squared himself up and hollered out, "I've told you, haven't I, how Brer Fox is the riding horse for our family? He started losing his gait lately, but I expect I can fetch him all right in a month or so," he said.

Everybody was talking and laughing, and Brer Rabbit smoked his cigar and allowed himself a little grin.

By and by, along towards night, Brer Rabbit said he'd better be going. He was asked to stay until after supper because he was such lively company, but he said his good-byes just the same. He strutted out to the horse rack as if he were king of the cats. Then he mounted Brer Fox, and they rode off.

Before long, Brer Rabbit figured that Brer Fox was cooking something up for him, because Brer Fox didn't have a word to say. He just kept his mouth shut and ambled along. It went on like this until Brer Fox was out of sight of Miss Meadows's house. Then he turned loose.

He ripped and roared, he cussed and swore. He tried to fling Brer Rabbit off his back, but he might as well have wrastled his own shadow. Every time he leapt, Brer Rabbit dug in with his spurs, and there they had it, up and down.

Brer Fox nearly tore up the ground. He jumped so high and he jumped so quick that he came mighty close to ripping his own tail off. They went on this way until by and by Brer Fox lay down and rolled over, and this sort of unsettled Brer Rabbit.

But by the time Brer Fox got back on his feet, Brer Rabbit was running lickety-clickety, clickety-lickety off through the underbrush like a racehorse. He ran and he ran, and after he'd been runnin' a mighty long time, he jumped up and cracked his heels together, and laughed fit to kill himself.

Brer Rabbit Jumps

Brer Bear

The Moon in the Millpond

THEN there were times when all the folks would go around just like they belonged to the same family and sagaciate together just like they'd never had a falling out.

One time after they'd been in cahoots this way, Brer Rabbit began to get uppity, he did, because the more peace they had, the worse he felt. By and by, he got restless in the mind. When the sun shone he'd go off and lay in the grass and kick at gnats and wallow in the sand.

One night after supper, while he was romancing around, he came upon old Brer Terrapin. Enough time had passed since their race that they could laugh about it, and they shook hands, and then they sat down by the side of the road and ran on about old times. They talked, and they talked, they did, until at last Brer Rabbit said, "The time's come to have some fun."

Brer Terrapin said, "Brer Rabbit's the very one I've been looking for," said he.

"Well, then," said Brer Rabbit, "we'll just give Brer Fox and Brer Wolf and Brer Bear notice. Tomorrow night we'll meet down by the millpond and have a little fishing frolic. I'll do the talking," said Brer Rabbit. "You can just sit back and agree," said he.

Brer Terrapin laughed. "If I ain't there," said he, "then you'll know a grasshopper done fly away with me," said he.

"Yes, sir," said Brer Rabbit, said he, "we'll put out the word that we're gonna romp and tromp 'til midnight, fish heads'll fill the air 'til daylight. I'll say we're gonna pitch a wang-dang-doodle all night long." Then he laughed, Brer Rabbit did, and he cocked an eye at Brer Terrapin, and he said, said he, "But you needn't bring no fiddle, 'cause there won't be no dancing there."

With that, Brer Rabbit put out for home and went to bed.

Brer Terrapin bruised around and inched his way toward the millpond so he could be there on time. "If you're slow, start early," said he.

The next day, Brer Rabbit got word to the other folks, and they were all put out only because they hadn't thought it up themselves. Brer Fox said he'd go fetch Miss Meadows and the other gals.

Sure enough, when the time came, they were all there. Brer Bear fetched a hook and line. Brer Fox fetched a dip net, and Brer Terrapin, not to be outdone, had fetched the bait.

Brer Bear said he'd try for catfish. Brer Wolf said he'd fish for horny-heads. Brer Fox said he'd go for perch, and Brer Rabbit winked at Brer Terrapin and said he was going to fish for suckers.

Brer Rabbit marched up to the pond and made like he was going to throw his hook in the water. But then he stopped. The other folks turned and watched him. He dropped his pole, he did, and he stood there scratching his head and looking down in the water.

The folks began to get uneasy when they saw this, and Miss Meadows up and hollered out, she did, "Law! Brer Rabbit! What in the name of goodness is the matter there?"

But Brer Rabbit kept on scratching and looking.

By and by, he fetched a long, deep breath, he did, and he said, "We just might as well make tracks from this here place, 'cause there ain't no fishing in that pond for none of this here crowd."

With that, Brer Terrapin scrambled up to the edge and looked over. He shook his head and said, "To be sure. Tut! Tut! Tut!" He crawled back, he did, and looked like he was thinking hard.

"Don't be scared, folks, cause we're bound to take care of you, let come what will," said Brer Rabbit, said he. "Accidents happen to us all. There ain't nothing much the matter, 'cepting that Mr. Moon done dropped in the water. If you don't believe me, you can look for yourself," said he.

With that, they all crowded along the bank and looked in. Sure enough, there was Mr. Moon, swinging and swaying at the bottom of the pond.

Brer Fox looked in, and he said, "Well, well, well."

Brer Wolf looked in, and he said, "Mighty bad, mighty bad."

Brer Bear looked in, and he said, "Tsk, tsk, tsk."

Miss Meadows looked in, and she squalled out, "Ain't that too much?"

Brer Rabbit looked in again, and he said, "You all can hem and haw, but unless we get that moon out of the pond, there won't be any fish caught tonight. Ask Brer Terrapin. He'll tell you the same."

"But how do we get that moon out of there?" they asked.

And Brer Terrapin said, "We'd better leave that to Brer Rabbit," said he.

Brer Rabbit rolled his eyes, he did, and made like he was working in his mind. By and by, he up and said, "The quickest way out of this here difficulty is to send 'round to old Brer Mud Turtle. We'll borrow his big net, and drag that moon up from there," said he.

"I'm mighty glad you thought of that," said Brer Terrapin, said he. "I trust you won't find him disaccounting."

Well, Brer Rabbit went after the big net. And while he was gone, Brer Terrapin said he heard time and time again that them that find the moon in the water and fetch it out will also fetch out a pot of money.

This made Brer Fox, Brer Wolf, and Brer Bear feel mighty good. They allowed, they did, that since Brer Rabbit was so kind as to run after the net, they would do the netting.

When Brer Rabbit got back, he saw how the land lay, and he made like he wanted to go in after Mr. Moon. He pulled off his coat, and he was fixing to shuck off his vest. But the other folks said they wouldn't hear of a dry-foot like Brer Rabbit going in the water. So Brer Fox, he took hold of one end of the net, and Brer Bear waded along behind to lift the net over the logs and snags.

They made one haul — no moon.

Another haul — no moon.

Yet another haul — no moon.

By and by, they got out further from the bank. Water ran in Brer Fox's ear. He shook his head. Water ran in Brer Wolf's ear. He shook his head. And the next thing you know, while they were a-shaking, they came to where the bottom shelved off. Brer Fox fell in and ducked himself. Then Brer Wolf ducked himself. And Brer Bear made a plunge and ducked himself, too. They kicked and splattered, splattered and kicked, until it looked like they were going to slosh all the water out of the millpond.

When they came out, Miss Meadows and the gals were all snickering, and well they might, because there couldn't be any worse-looking creatures.

Brer Rabbit hollered, "I 'spect you better go home and get on some dry duds, and another time we'll have better luck," said he. "I hear that the moon will bite at a hook if you use fools for bait, and I wager that's the only way to catch him," said he.

Brer Fox and Brer Wolf and Brer Bear went dripping off.

Brer Terrapin, he just laughed and laughed.

Brer Rabbit, he went home and capered around in the grass one half of the night, and played with the lightning bugs the other half.

Mr Moon Done Dropped in the Water

Hominy Grove

Music by Van Dyke Parks
Words by Van Dyke Parks and Martin F. Kibbee

1.,4. Off the__ wall,__ wall flow - er Now the dance has be - gun.__
2. You the__ wild,__ wild flow - er That my gar - den has grown.__
3. My whole heart's__ af - fec - tion Would I lay__ at your feet.__

It's our__ shin - ing hou - r 'Til all our dan - cin' is done__
How I__ in__ your pow - er And you a rake__ on your own__
Why one__ man's__ con - fec - tion Could be an - oth - er man's sweet__

__ Mam - my wham - my jam - my Cook - in' up__ on the stove For
__ Hot ten tot hot tod - dy Cin - na - mon__ and a clove For
__ Weave in my di - rec - tion When the web__ has been wove 'N

me and my but - ter cup Things have been look - in' up In Hom - in - y
lov - in' our lov - in' cup Things have been look - in' up In Hom - in - y
stick us to - geth - er like Birds__ of a fea - ther down In Hom - in - y

Grove____ Sweet Hom - in - y____ Grove.
Grove____ Sweet Hom - in - y____
Grove____ Sweet Hom - in - y____